PUFFIN BOOKS

FAT PUSS ON WHEELS

Fat Puss has some exciting adventures with his friends the
Mouse family, Humphrey Beaver and Christine Crow. He finds
himself baby-sitting up a tree, playing goalie in a football match
and roller-skating straight into the river! Life certainly is fun
with Fat Puss!

Harriet Castor was only twelve years old when she wrote her
first Fat Puss stories, *Fat Puss and Friends*, in 1983. Harriet is
now studying History at Cambridge University.

Also by Harriet Castor

FAT PUSS AND FRIENDS

Harriet Castor

Fat Puss
on Wheels

Illustrated by Colin West

Puffin Books

PUFFIN BOOKS

Published by the Penguin Group
Penguin Books Ltd, 27 Wrights Lane, London W8 5TZ, England
Viking Penguin, a division of Penguin Books USA Inc.
375 Hudson Street, New York, New York 10014, USA
Penguin Books Australia Ltd, Ringwood, Victoria, Australia
Penguin Books Canada Ltd, 2801 John Street, Markham, Ontario, Canada L3R 1B4
Penguin Books (NZ) Ltd, 182–190 Wairau Road, Auckland 10, New Zealand

Penguin Books Ltd, Registered Offices: Harmondsworth, Middlesex, England

First published by Viking Kestrel 1988
Published in Puffin Books 1989
10 9 8 7 6 5 4 3

Printed in England by Clays Ltd, St Ives plc

Contents

Fat Puss
on Wheels

One day, Fat Puss was
helping his friends, Robert and
Charlotte Mouse, to put some
rubbish on the rubbish dump.

"Look what I've found!"
Robert called out excitedly.

He held up a dirty piece of
metal with wheels on it.

"What is it?" asked Fat Puss.

"It's a roller-skate," said
Robert. "Can we play with it?"

"Well, I think we ought to
clean it first," said Fat Puss.

So Fat Puss, Robert and
Charlotte took the roller-skate
home and cleaned it until it was
bright and shiny. Then they had
great fun playing with it.

Robert and Charlotte sat on the
roller-skate and Fat Puss pulled
them along.

When Fat Puss got tired, they
pushed themselves along with
sticks instead.

"Why don't you try riding on it, Fat Puss?" they called.

"All right," said Fat Puss. He managed to sit on the roller-skate, but when Robert and Charlotte tried to pull him along, they just couldn't move him at all.

"Try pushing yourself along with a stick," suggested Charlotte.

But the stick snapped.

"Why don't you lie on your tummy and push yourself along with your paws?" said Robert.

But Fat Puss fell off.

"Perhaps it would be easier if
you started at the top of a hill,"
said Charlotte.

"Yes," agreed Robert.

So Fat Puss took the roller-skate to the top of a hill and sat on it again. Sure enough, he began to move.

"Isn't it wonderful?" cried the mice.

"Yes," shouted Fat Puss. The roller-skate started to go faster and faster. "But how do I stop?"

"Oh, dear," said Robert,
"there's a river at the bottom of
that hill."

Fat Puss hung on to the roller-
skate and shut his eyes . . .

SPLOSH! He landed in the river.

Luckily, it wasn't very deep.

"Are you all right?" called the mice.

"Yes," replied Fat Puss. He tried to get up. "Except that I'm stuck in the mud!"

"Oh, no," said Robert. "What shall we do now?"

"I think we'd better get Mummy and Daddy," said Charlotte.

So the Mouse children left
Fat Puss sitting in the river, and
they ran to fetch Jessica and
Terence. Terence asked
Humphrey Beaver to come and
help too, and Jessica fetched a
piece of rope. Then they all
went back to Fat Puss.

"Don't worry, Fat Puss," said
Terence. "We'll get you out."
Humphrey jumped into the
river and tied one end of the
rope around Fat Puss's tummy.

Then all the mice pulled on the other end, while Humphrey pushed Fat Puss from behind.

"Pull! Pull!" shouted
Terence.

At last, with a squelch, Fat
Puss came out of the mud and

everyone fell over.

Fat Puss climbed on to the riverbank, covered in mud.

"I think you need a bath," laughed Terence.

"Yes," said Fat Puss. "Thank you for getting me out."

"But where's the roller-skate?" asked Robert and Charlotte.

"I'm afraid that got stuck in the mud too," said Fat Puss.

"And I think it ought to stay there," said Humphrey, "so that we don't have any more accidents."

Footballer
Fat Puss

One morning, Terence Mouse
visited Fat Puss. Terence looked
rather worried.

"What's the matter?" asked
Fat Puss.

"Well," said Terence. "We are supposed to be playing a football match tomorrow with the Rabbit family, but we need five players and there are only four of us. Would you play with us?"

"Of course," replied Fat Puss.
Terence looked relieved. "But
I've never played in a football
match before."

"That doesn't matter," said
Terence. "We've got all day to
teach you."

30

So for the rest of the day, the Mouse family taught Fat Puss to play football. Robert and Charlotte helped him to practise running as fast as he could.

Jessica taught him how to
kick a ball.

And Terence explained
the rules of the game
to him. That evening Fat Puss
felt very tired and a little
nervous about the match.

The next morning, the Mouse
family went to see Fat Puss,
who was looking rather upset.

"Are you all right, Fat Puss?" asked Terence.

"No," sobbed Fat Puss. "Because of all that training yesterday, I feel stiff all over and I can hardly walk, let alone run."

"Oh, no," said Jessica. "What shall we do?"

"I'm so sorry that I've let everyone down," said Fat Puss.

"But you haven't!"
exclaimed Terence. "I've had
an idea. I don't know why we
didn't think of it before. Why
don't we let Fat Puss be the
goalkeeper? He's so big that he
won't have to move around
very much."

"That's a wonderful idea,"
said Jessica.

So the mice helped Fat Puss
to get to the football match,
and when it started, he stood in
the goal.

He found that he didn't need
to move at all because the ball
simply bounced off his tummy.

39

After the match all the mice hugged Fat Puss.

"You were so good," said Terence, "that we've decided to make you a permanent member of the team."

"Oh, thank you," said Fat Puss.

He was proud to be in the team and very happy that he hadn't let his friends down after all.

Flying
Fat Puss

One sunny day, Fat Puss and
his friends, the Mouse family,
decided to go for a picnic. They

all helped to pack the food in a
basket and then they went to
the park.

43

In the park, the Mouse children played hide-and-seek. Fat Puss joined in, although he wasn't very good at it. First he tried hiding behind a tree and

then he tried hiding under a pile
of leaves, but Robert and
Charlotte always found him
straight away.

While she was looking for
somewhere to hide, Charlotte
found a big bunch of shiny
balloons tied to a tree. She
untied one, and ran to show it
to the others.

But suddenly she found that
she wasn't on the ground any
more. She was flying!

"Look at me!" she cried and then came back to earth with a little bump. "It's great fun!"

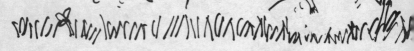

The other mice ran to get a
balloon and they found that
they could fly too. But Fat Puss
couldn't fly.

He held his balloon tightly,
and ran as fast as he could, but
he just couldn't get off the
ground.

"Never mind, Fat Puss," said Terence. "I think it's time we had our picnic."

"Oh, yes!" cried Robert and Charlotte.

"But we should put the balloons back first," said Jessica.

"Oh, I'll do that," said Fat Puss.

Everyone gave their balloons
to Fat Puss and he hurried over
to the tree.

Before he got there, he began
to feel rather strange. His feet
weren't on the ground any
more. He was flying at last! He

went up and up until he was as
high as the treetops, and he
looked around at the wonderful
view.

As he drifted past a tree, he met Christine Crow. She was very surprised to see Fat Puss floating by.

Fat Puss was beginning to feel rather worried. "How shall I get down again?" he asked her.

"That is a problem," said Christine, "because if you just let go, you'll fall and hurt yourself." She thought for a moment. Then she had an idea.

"I know what to do," she said.

Christine popped one of the balloons with her beak.

Fat Puss sank down a little.
Then she popped another. Fat
Puss sank a little more.

Christine popped another,
and gradually Fat Puss sank all
the way back to the ground.

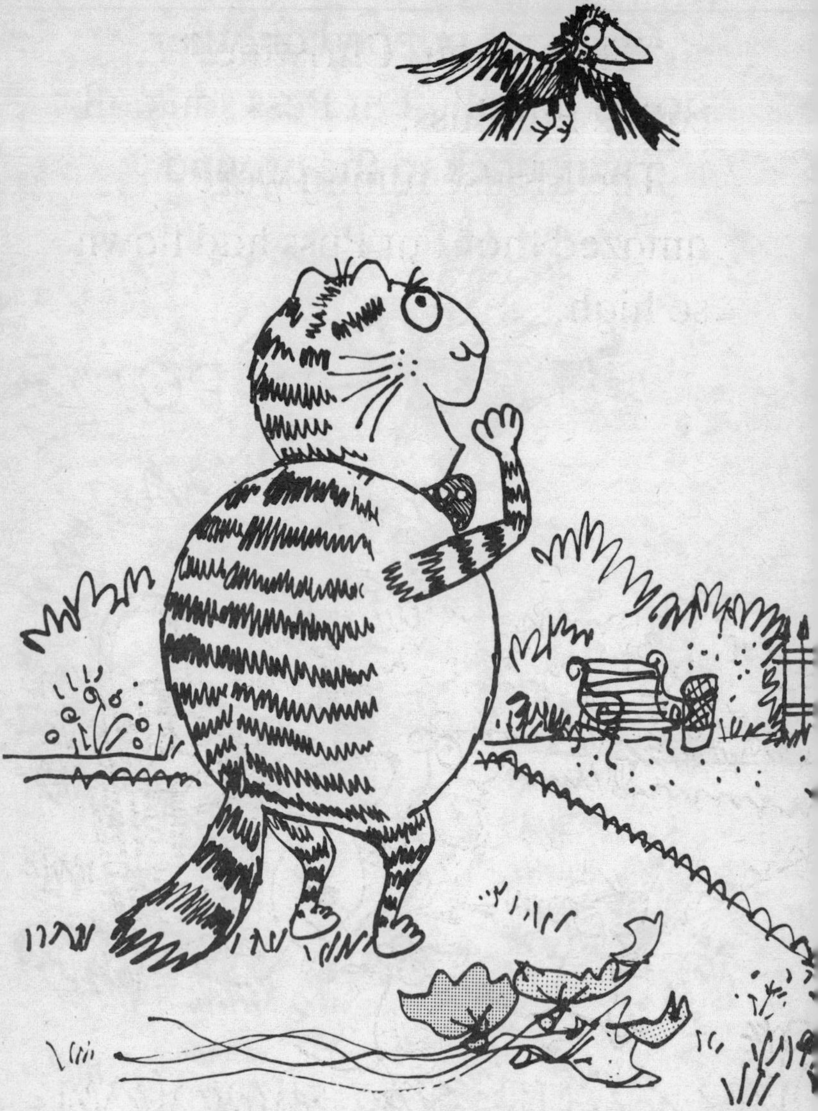

"Thank you, Christine," called Fat Puss.

The Mouse family were amazed that Fat Puss had flown so high.

"What does everything look like from up there?" asked Robert and Charlotte excitedly.

"Come on," said Terence. "Fat Puss will tell us all about it in a minute. But first we really must have our picnic!"

Fat Puss and
the Baby Crows

One day, Christine Crow
came to see Fat Puss.

"I'm going to my sister's birthday party tonight," she said. "But I need someone to look after Katie, Lizzie and Kevin, my three babies, while I'm out. Would you mind looking after them for me, Fat Puss?"

"I'd love to!" said Fat Puss, feeling very proud that Christine had asked him.

So, that evening, Fat Puss
went to the tree where Christine
lived. Her nest was quite a long
way up.

"How will I get up there?" asked Fat Puss.

"Oh, dear, I didn't think of that," said Christine. "Aren't you very good at climbing trees?"

"Not really," replied Fat Puss.

"I'd better give you some help then," said Christine. "But I don't think I can manage it on my own. I know, I'll go and fetch Grandma Crow." And off she flew.

Very soon, Christine came
back with Grandma Crow.

"Now, Fat Puss," said
Christine, "Grandma and I will
help you. Don't worry."

But Fat Puss was worried.
He'd never climbed a tree
before.

First Christine and Grandma
Crow pulled him by his front
paws . . .

. . . and then they pushed him
up from behind.

Slowly, Fat Puss got from one branch to another, and before long he reached the nest.

"Well done!" chirped the baby birds.

Fat Puss could only just fit
into the nest, so Katie, Lizzie
and Kevin snuggled down on
his big, furry tummy.

Then Christine said
"Goodbye," and went off to the
party with Grandma Crow.

Fat Puss started to tell the
baby birds a bedtime story.

After a little while, it became
dark. Fat Puss started to feel
scared. He didn't like the dark.
Suddenly an owl hooted, and
Fat Puss almost fell out of the
nest with shock.

"What's the matter?" asked the baby birds.

"I – I'm scared," said Fat Puss.

"It's all right, Fat Puss," said Lizzie. "It was only an owl."

But Fat Puss still looked very worried. "I'm afraid of the dark," he whispered.

"Never mind," said Katie. "We'll sing to you to make you feel better."

"Yes, that's a good idea!" said Kevin.

So the three little birds
started to sing, and very soon
Fat Puss stopped being scared
and began to feel sleepy
instead.

When Christine Crow came home later that night, she found all four of them cuddled together, fast asleep.

Fat Puss
on Holiday

It was summer, and Fat Puss
decided to go on holiday.

"Where shall I go?" he asked
Terence Mouse.

"What about the seaside?"
suggested Terence.

"That's a good idea," said
Fat Puss. "But what could I do
there?"

"Oh, lots of things," replied
Terence. "You could build
sandcastles, and collect shells,
and swim in the sea."

"That sounds wonderful!"
said Fat Puss.

So Fat Puss got out his
suitcase, and the Mouse family
helped him to pack. They put in
Fat Puss's toothbrush, Fat
Puss's pyjamas and Fat Puss's
straw hat.

Then Fat Puss said goodbye
to the mice and to Humphrey
Beaver, and off he went to the
seaside.

Fat Puss spent all day
building a beautiful sandcastle,
collecting lots of interesting
shells and swimming in the
warm, blue sea.

The sun was shining brightly,
and he felt very happy. "Oh, I
love being on holiday," he said.

But the next day, Fat Puss found that the sea had washed his beautiful sandcastle away, and where his pile of shells had been he found only a rather grumpy crab, who pinched his paw.

The sky was cloudy and grey,
and when he swam in the sea, it
was very cold.

Fat Puss felt homesick. He didn't want to build sandcastles any more. He wanted to roll down hills like he did at home.

He didn't want to collect shells
any more. He wanted to talk to
the Mouse family. He didn't
want to swim in the sea any
more. He wanted to swim in the
river with Humphrey Beaver.

So Fat Puss put his toothbrush, his pyjamas and his straw hat back in his suitcase, and he set off home.

As soon as Fat Puss got
home, he rolled down a hill.

Then he went to see the Mouse family. And then he went for a swim in the river with Humphrey Beaver.

"Did you enjoy going on holiday, Fat Puss?" asked Humphrey.

"Oh, yes, thank you," replied Fat Puss. "But I like coming home even more."